Beauty and the Beast

Adapted from the film by
A. L. SINGER

Hippo Books
Scholastic Children's Books
London

Scholastic Children's Books,
Scholastic Publications Ltd,
7–9 Pratt Street, London NW1 0AE

Scholastic Inc.,
730 Broadway, New York, NY 10003, USA

Scholastic Canada Ltd,
123 Newkirk Road, Richmond Hill,
Ontario, Canada L4C 3G5

Ashton Scholastic Pty Ltd,
P O Box 579, Gosford, New South Wales,
Australia

Ashton Scholastic Ltd,
Private Bag 1, Penrose, Auckland,
New Zealand

First published in the US by Disney Press 1992
First published in the UK by Scholastic Publications Ltd, 1992

Text and illustrations copyright © Disney Press 1992

ISBN 0 590 55123 X

Typeset in Plantin by Contour Typesetters, Southall, London
Printed by Cox & Wyman, Reading, Berks

10 9 8 7 6 5 4 3

LIST OF COLOUR PLATES

11 "By the way, thank you for saving my life," Belle murmurs.

12 "Impress her with your delightful wit! Shower her with compliments," Lumiere advises the Beast.

13 In the Beasts's lair, Belle discovers an enchanted rose.

14 The enraged Beast catches Belle and snatches the rose away.

15 The household objects brace themselves for the attack of Gaston and the townspeople.

16 Lumiere rescues the pretty feather duster during the fray.

1

$\mathcal{O}$nce upon a time in a faraway land there was a magical kingdom where just about everything was perfect. The land was green, the people were happy, the castle was majestic.

The young Prince, however was another story.

He had grown up with everything he desired, yet his heart remained cold. He was selfish, spoiled, and unkind. Yet because he was the Prince, no one dared say no to him. No one dared to try to teach him a lesson.

Until one bitterly cold, raw, winter night.

On that night, an old beggar woman came to the castle, shivering and weak. The servants led her to the Prince. She bowed to him, taking a red rose from her basket.

"Kind sir," she said, "would you grant me shelter from the cold? I regret I have no money, but I can offer you this small, perfect rose as a token of my gratitude."

The servants had taken pity on the poor woman, but the Prince saw only her filth and ugliness. "Be gone, you foul beggar," he said. "And look not at my mirrors on the way out, lest they crack in horror!"

"My lord," the woman said, "do not be fooled by my outward appearance. For beauty is found within all things."

"I see," replied the Prince. "Then find beauty within someone else's house!" He turned to his servants. "Take this old bag of bones away, I say!"

But before the servants could touch her, she began to glow with a powerful light. As they looked on in awe, the old woman was transformed into a beautiful enchantress.

The Prince shook with fright. In the eyes of this enchantress, he could see an anger that was terrifying. "Please forgive me," he cried, dropping to his knees. "I . . . I didn't know—"

But she wouldn't let him finish. "I have seen that there is no love in your heart," she said. "That makes you no better than a beast—and so you shall *become* a beast!"

"No!" the Prince protested. "Please . . ."

The enchantress raised her hands high. Slowly the boy changed. Dark hair sprouted on his face and hands. Claws grew from his fingertips. He screamed with pain as his teeth became long and sharp.

"I hereby cast a spell on the entire castle," the

enchantress declared. "You shall remain a prisoner here—and you shall have no human company."

Instantly, everyone else in the castle changed too. The head of the household, Cogsworth, became a mantel clock. The maître d', Lumiere, became a candelabra. The cook, Mrs. Potts, became a teapot. Others became furniture, china, even silverware—until not one human being was left.

The enchantress then held up the rose. "This rose will bloom until your twenty-first birthday, and then it will wither and die. You have until then to break the spell. If you don't you will be doomed to remain a beast forever."

"But how can I break the spell?" said the frightened boy-beast. His voice was now a raspy snarl.

The enchantress leaned closer to him. "The only way to break it is to love another person and earn that person's love in return."

She placed the rose in a bell jar on a table, then pulled a small silver mirror out of her basket. "I also leave you with a gift. This enchanted mirror will show you any part of the world you wish to see. Look well, for it is a world you can no longer be part of!"

Then, in a flash of light, the enchantress disappeared.

The Beast stomped out of the room and ran up the stairs of the castle tower. Up, up, up he climbed, tripping over his new, clumsy, hairy feet. When he

3

finally reached the top, he looked out of the tower window.

He was shocked by what he saw. There was not one person in the castle grounds, not one house, not one road, not one grassy field. The sunny countryside had been swallowed up by a thick, grey mist.

He had to earn another person's love. That was what the enchantress had said.

"But who on Earth could learn to love a beast?" the boy thought in despair.

He reared his head back and howled. It was the howl of a caged animal. It was the howl of a boy who had lost everything.

2

*F*ar away from where the castle now lay hidden was a charming little village. And in that village was a girl more beautiful than any other girl in the land. Her name was Belle. She was so lovely that when she walked through her tiny village, everyone noticed. The baker, the blacksmith, the fruit seller, the milkmaid—even the children would stop what they were doing to watch her pass.

But Belle was unaware of their glances. She was always too busy reading. She even read while she walked.

"All that beauty," the villagers would say, shaking their heads. "It's a shame she's not normal. She always has her head buried in a book. She's just as strange as her father."

To Belle, there was nothing strange about reading. In books there was adventure, romance, excitement. There were dangers and Prince Charmings and happy endings. Books were more interesting than her dull, humdrum village, where every day was the same as the day before.

As for her father, Maurice, well, Belle was very proud of him. To her, he was the most clever inventor in the whole world. True, he was a bit forgetful. True, his inventions never seemed to work exactly the way they were supposed to. But Belle knew he would prove himself to the world someday.

And when he did, maybe he would take her away from this small town. Maybe he would take her somewhere glamorous and exciting where she could meet her own Prince Charming.

But till then, she would have to wait—and read— and fight off the foolish men who tried to win her love.

Like Gaston.

Gaston was a fine, handsome hunter, admired by many of the young women in town. He was also a braggart, a coward, and a cheat.

One Autumn day, as Belle walked through the town square, reading, Gaston said to his constant companion, Lefou, "There she is, Lefou. She's the lucky girl I'm going to marry."

"The inventor's daughter?" said Lefou. "The one with her nose in a book? She's odd. She's . . ."

"She's the most beautiful girl in town," Gaston added. "And don't I deserve the best?"

"Of course . . . I mean, yes, but . . ." Lefou stuttered.

Gaston ran after Belle with Lefou following close behind. When Gaston caught up with her, just outside the marketplace, he slowed down. "Hello Belle," he announced with a cocky smile.

Belle barely glanced up from her book. "Hello Gaston," she answered.

Gaston grabbed Belle's book out of her hand. "My dear, it's not right for a girl to read. It's time you got your head out of these books and paid attention to more important things—like me."

"Gaston, may I have my book please?" Belle said, trying to control her anger.

Gaston grinned and threw her book into a mud puddle. "How about walking over to the tavern and looking at my trophies?"

He gripped her arm but Belle shook it loose. "Please, Gaston," she said, furious that he had ruined her book. "I have to get home to help my father. Good-bye!" She picked up her book and began walking away.

As Lefou approached, he muttered with a sneer, "Your father? That crazy old loon. He needs all the help he can get."

Belle spun around. "Don't talk about my father like that! He's a genius!"

But before she could say anything else—BOOOOOOM!—an explosion shook the ground.

A plume of smoke rose from a small house just up the road.

7

Belle's house!

"Papa!" Belle screamed. She ran home as fast as she could.

When she pulled open the door of her father's workshop, thick smoke billowed out. In the midst of it, sitting beside a broken hulk of wooden slats and metal gears, was her father, Maurice.

She ran to his side. "Are you all right, Papa?"

Coughing and muttering, Maurice stood up and kicked his invention. "How on Earth did that happen? I'll never get this irritating contraption to work!"

Belle smiled, relieved that he wasn't hurt. "Oh, yes you will," she said. "And you'll win first prize at the fair tomorrow—*and* become a world-famous inventor."

"Do you really believe that?" Maurice said, a small smile flickering across his face.

"I always have," Belle said confidently.

"Well, then, what are we waiting for?" Maurice said, grabbing a tool. "I'll have this thing fixed in no time!"

As Belle watched him work, she began thinking. Gaston's mocking words came back to her: "*It's not right for a girl to read.*"

"Papa," she said, "do you think I'm odd?"

Maurice popped out from behind his invention, his glases crooked, his hair standing on end. "My daughter? Odd? Now where would you get that idea?"

"I don't know, I'm just not sure I fit in here," Belle said. She looked at her father sadly. "Oh, Papa, I want excitement and adventure in my life . . . and I want someone to share it with."

Belle's voice had grown soft with that last comment. Her father nodded knowingly. "Well, how about that Gaston? He's a handsome fellow."

"He's not for me, Papa," Belle said. "He's crude and conceited."

"Well, don't worry. This invention's going to be the start of a new life for us." Maurice gave his daughter a warm smile. "Then we'll leave this place and you can have a chance at those dreams."

Before long, Maurice had the contraption working again, with plenty of time left to take it to the fair. Belle helped him load it into a wooden wagon, then they hitched the wagon to their horse, Philippe. Slinging a cape around his shoulders, Maurice mounted the horse and set off.

"Goode-bye!" Belle shouted, waving after him. "Good luck!"

As Philippe trotted down the road, Maurice held a map tightly, making sure to follow the correct route. It wasn't until three hours later that he realized something awful.

9

The map was upside down.

Maurice groaned. Nothing around him looked familiar. "Now we'll never make it to the fair," he said. "Belle will be so disappointed."

Philippe slowly approached a fork in the road. There was a sign there, but the words on it had faded.

To the left, the road continued along a river. To the right, it disappeared into a thick, misty forest. Maurice peered up both roads, then pulled Philippe to the right.

Philippe reared back and shook his head.

But Maruice just pulled harder. "Come on, Philippe. It's a shortcut. We'll be there in no time."

Philippe went to the right, into the forest. The road grew narrower and trees made black shadows on the ground. Slowly, a thick, gray fog settled over them. The drip, drip, drip of water from a tree echoed in the dead silence.

A sharp wind whistled through the gnarled branches, causing them to twitch like sharp, bony fingers. Maurice held his jacket closed against the sudden cold.

Then a long shadow skittered among the trees, rustling the leaves. Philippe stopped. He looked around fearfully.

"Uh, we'd better turn around . . ." Maurice began.

But it was too late. A pair of pale yellow eyes

10

appeared in the brush. Philippe whinnied, rearing up on his hind legs.

"Whoa, Philippe!" Maurice yelled, but he couldn't hold on. He tumbled to the ground as Philippe galloped away.

"Philippe?" Maurice whispered into the darkness. He got up quickly and looked around frantically. Again, he saw the yellow eyes, and hoped against hope that they belonged to something friendly.

But there was nothing friendly about the animal's angry growl, or its long, sharp, glistening teeth.

It was a wolf!

3

*R*rrrrrrrrr . . .

   Maurice backed away from the wolf's growl. "N-n-no," he muttered. "No!"

The wolf sprang towards him. Maurice turned and ran. He crashed through the undergrowth, ignoring the branches that lashed his face.

Then he saw another shadow, and another. It was a whole pack of wolves! Maurice ran left, then right. The wolves were panting, snarling. He looked back to see many pairs of yellow eyes gaining on him.

And that was when a dim, far-off light caught his eye. He raced towards it. But the trees became thicker. Thorns ripped his trousers, branches seemed to push him back like arms.

Then he smacked against something hard. Metallic. A gate! "Help!" he cried out. "Is someone there? Help!"

The gate creaked open.

Maurice raced through, then slammed it shut after

him. Seconds later, with a loud crash, the wolves hurled themselves against the gate and fell away.

Maurice heaved a sigh of relief. His heart was beating furiously. He turned around, hoping to find that light.

What he saw took his breath away.

He had found the light, all right. It was coming from an enormous castle. A dark, old, crumbling castle surrounded by mist.

It looked as though no one had taken care of the castle for ages. Yet the light meant someone was inside, so Maurice walked towards it.

He crossed over a bridge. Below him was a dried-up moat. On the other side of the bridge, weeds and vines covered the castle grounds. They crept up garden walls and tangled around broken marble statues.

Just then a thunderbolt split the sky, casting a harsh white light over the castle, and instantly rain began to fall in torrents.

Light still flickered through the castle's open door, so Maurice stepped cautiously inside.

On a table just inside the door there was a beautiful, lighted candelabra and a mantel clock. Beyond them was the largest room Maurice had ever seen. Rich-looking but tattered tapestries hung from the walls. Tarnished and chipped statues stood in corners. The floors were covered with thick, dusty carpets. Dark

13

archways led to dark, faraway rooms.

Staring with wonder, Maurice managed to call out, "Hello?"

His voice echoed in the dim parlour.

Then he heard voices. The first said, "Poor fellow must have lost his way, Cogsworth."

The second snapped, "Keep quiet, Lumiere. Maybe he'll go away."

"Oh, have a heart," came the first voice. Then, louder, it said. "You are welcome here, monsieur!"

"Who said that?" Maurice asked. "Where are you?"

Maurice felt something tugging at his cloak. He whirled around but saw no one.

"Down here!" said the second voice.

When Maurice looked down, his eyes grew wide. The *mantel clock* was tugging at him! It had arms and legs—and a face!

"I am Monsieur Cogsworth," the clock said, in a manner that was not very friendly.

Then the candelabra spoke with a welcoming voice. "And I am Monsieur Lumiere, at your service."

"You're . . . you're alive!" Maurice said, picking up Cogsworth and poking him. "How can that be?"

"Please put me down, sir," Cogsworth said, "or I shall give you a sound thrashing!"

Maurice obeyed, saying, "I beg your pardon, it's

14

just that—AAAAAAH-CHOO!" The sneeze exploded out of him.

"You are soaked to the bone, monsieur," Lumiere said. "Come warm yourself by the fire."

"No!" Cogsworth retorted. "I forbit it! The master will be furious if he finds him here!"

But Lumiere ignored him, pulling Maurice into a spacious drawing room where a roaring fire gave off a warm, amber glow. Maurice settled himself in a comfortable leather armchair. A footstool, yapping happily like a dog, scooted under Maurice's feet.

"Well, hello there boy!" Maurice said.

"Oh, no, no, no, no, no no!" Cogsworth cried, putting his hands over his eyes. "I am not seeing this!"

A tea cart rolled into the room. On it was a round teapot with a plump, friendly face, and a small chipped teacup.

"I'm Mrs. Potts and this is my son Chip," she said. "Would you like a spot of hot tea, sir?"

"No!" Cogsworth shouted. "No tea!"

"Yes, please," said Maurice gratefully.

As Mrs. Potts poured tea, Cogsworth grabbed Lumiere. "We've got to get him out of here! You know what the master will do if . . ."

"Calm yourself," Lumiere said. "The master will never have to know. Now hush, our guest is falling asleep."

Cogsworth sputtered with frustration. But Maurice

was indeed falling into a deep, blissful sleep . . .

WHAMMMM!

The door flew open and Maurice jumped in his chair. The footstool yelped and scrambled under a table. The tea cart quickly rolled away, and Cogsworth dashed under a carpet.

Maurice spun around. There was someone—something—standing in the doorway. It towered on thick, hairy legs, and its head and arms were covered with matted fur. As it stepped towards Maurice, its feet pounded the floor like mallets. Under thick, tangled brows, its eyes glared angrily and its nostrils flared. "There's a stranger here," he growled.

Maurice wanted to run, but he couldn't. He was so frightened he froze to the spot.

Lumiere stepped forward quickly. "Master," he said, "you see, the gentleman was lost in the woods, so . . ."

"RRRRRAAAAGGGGGHHH!" The force of the Beast's roar blew out Lumiere's candles.

Cogsworth peered out from under the carpet. "I was against it from the start," he said. "I tried to . . ."

The Beast sneered at Maurice. "What are you doing here?"

"I was lost in the woods," Maurice answered, his eyes wide with fright, "and I . . ."

"What are you staring at?" the Beast demanded.

"N-n-nothing," Maurice stammered.

16

"You come into my home and stare at me!" the Beast accused.

Maurice bolted for the door, but the Beast blocked his way. "I meant no harm," Maurice said. "I just needed a place to stay."

The Beast grabbed Maurice by the shirt with his claws. In a sinister voice that made Maurice's blood run cold, he said, "I'll give you a place to stay!"

Right then, the only thing Maurice could think of was Belle.

He had a strange feeling that he would never see her again.

4

$\mathcal{G}$aston and Lefou walked briskly down the road from town. They wore their finest formal clothing. Behind them was a priest, a brass band, and just about every person who lived there.

When they reached Belle's house, Gaston turned. He held up his hands and everyone stopped. "Ladies and gentlemen, I'd like to thank you all for coming to my wedding! But first," he said, chuckling, "I'd better go in there and propose to the girl!"

The crowd laughed. Gaston marched to Belle's door and knocked hard.

Inside, Belle was reading. She put down her book, went to the door, and opened it a crack. "Gaston, what a pleasant surprise," she said, trying to hide her disappointment.

Gaston pushed the door open and barged in. "You know, Belle," he announced, "there's not a girl in town who wouldn't love to be in your shoes. This is the day your dreams come true!"

18

"What do *you* know about my dreams?" Belle said.

Gaston plopped down on Belle's chair and plonked his muddy boots on the table—right on her book. "Picture this," he said. "A rustic hunting lodge. My latest kill roasting on the fire. And my little wife massaging my feet while her little ones play on the floor—six or seven of them. And do you know who that little wife will be? You, Belle!"

Belle's jaw fell open in shock. He was proposing to her—and he had invited the whole town to watch! The nerve!

He stood up and tried to throw his arms around Belle. But she backed away towards the door, thinking frantically. "Gaston, I'm . . . I'm . . . speechless! I don't know what to say!"

Gaston followed her in a circle around the room, finally pinning her to the door. "Say you'll marry me!"

"Well, I'm really sorry, Gaston," Belle said, groping behind her for the doorknob, "but . . . Um, I . . . I just don't deserve you. But thanks for asking!"

She found the doorknob and pushed. As the door opened, she ducked out of the way. Gaston lost his balance and tumbled out.

She slammed the door shut just as Gaston landed in a mud puddle.

The crowd fell silent. Lefou walked slowly up to Gaston. "She turned you down, did she?" he said.

19

Gaston got up, furious. His fists were clenched, his eyes were burning. Nervously, people began to back away.

Then, suddenly, Gaston burst into laughter. "Turn *me* down? Nonsense! She's just playing hard to get!"

Smiling, with his head held high, he strode back to town.

The crowd stood silently, watching him. Many of them admired his dignity. Many of them wanted to laugh.

But not one them could see the expression on his face change. None of them could see the smile quickly turn into a fierce, angry grimace.

And none of them could hear his solemn vow: "I'll have Belle for my wife. One way or another."

Belle stayed in her house until every last person had left. "Imagine me, the wife of that brainless fool," she said to herself. As she opened the door to take a walk, she heard a familiar noise—Philippe's whinny.

"Papa?" she thought. "Back so soon?"

But when she looked up the road, she saw Philippe was alone. She ran towards him, crying out, "Philippe! What's the matter? Where's Papa?"

Philippe snorted and whinnied anxiously.

Belle was terrified. "We have to find him! Take me to him!"

She leapt on Philippe, and he galloped down the

road. Carefully he retraced his steps until they came to the forest, which was as dark and creepy as before. But this time Philippe was determined to make it through. The wind howled and whistled, pushing branches in his path, but he trudged onwards.

Belle felt her skin crawl. In her worst nightmares she had never imagined a place so horrible.

Suddenly, at the sight of the rusted gate, Philippe began to buck anxiously. "Steady, Philippe," Belle said. She hopped off and pulled him towards the gate. Pushing it open, she spotted a hat lying on the ground.

It was her father's hat.

"Papa!" she cried. "Come on Philippe!" She dragged the horse into the castle grounds, barely noticing the surroundings. Tying Philippe to a post, she ran into the castle.

"Papa?" she called out as she entered the grand hall. She ran through it and up a curved marble staircase. "Papa, are you here? It's Belle!"

When she reached the top of the stairs, Belle ran down a corridor—right past Cogsworth and Lumiere.

Cogsworth was frozen with surprise. Lumiere burst into tears. "A girl!" he cried. "A beautiful girl! After all these years, she's come to fall in love with the master and break the spell. Soon we will be human again!"

"Nonsense!" Cosgworth snapped. "She's here

because of that fellow locked in the tower. He must be her father."

"Then we must help her!" Lumiere said. He ran through the castle, taking a shortcut to get ahead of belle. He stopped in the corridor that led to the tower stairs.

Belle reached the stairs. When she saw Lumiere's flickering light, she called out, "Hello? Is someone there? I'm looking for . . ."

Lumiere moved up the stairs, then sat on a small shelf. Belle quickly followed him. When she got to the top she looked around, puzzled. There was a candleabra and a row of doors with small slots at the bottom. "That's funny," she said. "I'm sure there was somone . . ."

"Belle?"

The voice that called her was hoarse, but she knew exactly who it was. "Papa!" she screamed. "Where are you?"

Maurice's face peered through the bars in one of the doors. "Here." He reached his hand through the bars.

Belle ran to the door and grasped his hand. "Oh, Papa, your poor hands are like ice," she said. "We have to get you out of there!"

Shivering, Maurice said, "I don't know how you found me, Belle, but I want you to leave at once."

"Who's done this to you?" Belle demanded.

"No time to explain!" Maurice said, "You must go. Now!"

"No, Papa, I won't leave you!" Belle vowed.

Suddenly Belle felt darkness settle over her. She thought the candelabra had flickered out.

But when she turned around, she realized the darkness was a shadow. The shadow of someone enormous, someone she couldn't see.

"Who's there?" she said.

But the Beast didn't answer, not at first. He couldn't. The words wouldn't come. He felt ashamed of his ugliness as he stared at the most beautiful human being he had ever seen.

"Who are you?" Belle asked, as she peered into the darkness.

Softly, the Beast said, "The master of this castle."

"I've come for my father," Belle pleaded. "There must be some misunderstanding. Please let him out. He's sick!"

"He shouldn't have trespassed!" the Beast replied.

Belle struggled to see the face of her father's captor. "Please, I'll do anything to save his life," she said. "Take me instead!"

Silence hung in the air. The Beast looked at Belle carefully. Her hair, her eyes, her lovely face, made him feel warm inside. It was the first time he had felt like that in years. "You would take his place?" he asked.

23

"Belle, no!" Maurice shouted. "You don't know what you're doing!"

"If I did take his place," Belle continued, "would you let him go?"

"Yes," the Beast answered, "but you must promise to remain here forever."

The corridor froze with silence again. Belle thought for a moment. Who was this man? She needed to know desperately before she could give an answer. "Come into the light," she said.

The Beast stood still. He was ashamed to show his face in the presence of such perfect beauty.

But a desperate hope glimmered inside the Beast. Maybe, just maybe, she wouldn't mind what she saw. Maybe she would like him.

Slowly, he moved into the light.

Belle's eyes widened. She gasped with horror and turned away.

"No, Belle!" Maurice said. "I won't let you!"

But Belle was gathering her strength. She knew there was only one thing to do, as dreadful as it seemed.

She turned to face the Beast. "You have my word."

"Done!" the Beast said. And he quickly unlocked the door and began dragging Maurice out of the castle. Belle screamed and Maurice struggled, but he couldn't break the Beast's iron grip. "Please spare my daughter," he pleaded. "She had no part in this!"

24

But the Beast didn't even hear him. As he forced Maurice off the castle grounds, there was only one thought on the Beast's mind.

He had the girl all to himself now. Forever.

5

$\mathcal{N}$ow that Belle was locked in the tower, the Beast had no idea what to do with her. He mumbled to himself, pacing back and forth beneath the tower stairs. "After all these years . . . after I'd given up . . . what do I say to her?"

Lumiere watched him for a long time. He wanted so much for the Beast to do the right thing. Maybe, just maybe, the Beast could make Belle fall in love with him. And if he did, the spell would finally be broken.

It was the only hope for Lumiere, and for all the other servants, to become human again.

Gathering up his courage, Lumiere said, "Uh, master, since the girl is going to be with us for quite some time, perhaps you should offer her a more comfortable room."

The Beast growled, and Lumiere backed away in fright.

Then, muttering again, the Beast began to climb

26

Above: "You're . . . you're alive!" Maurice meets the enchanted objects who live in the Beast's castle.

Below: But who on earth could learn to love a Beast?

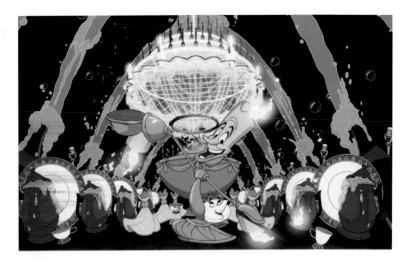

Above: "And now we invite you to relax and pull up a chair as the dining room proudly presents – your dinner!"

Below: Each time the kitchen door swung open, a plate of food came out, more delicious than the last.

Above: "All that beauty . . . It's a shame she's not normal. She always has her head buried in a book." The townspeople despair of Belle.

Below: "There she is, Lefou. She's the lucky girl I'm going to marry," boasts Gaston.

Above: "You'll win first prize at the fair tomorrow – and become a world-famous inventor," Belle promises Maurice.

Below: Maurice finds a light in the forest, coming from an enormous castle. A dark, old, crumbling castle surrounded by mist.

Above: "She doesn't shudder when she touches my paw any more," the Beast thinks to himself.

Below: Gaston fired an arrow. It sliced through the air and landed firmly in the Beast's shoulder.

Above: "By the way, thank you for saving my life," Belle murmurs.

Below: "Impress her with your delightful wit! Shower her with compliments," Lumiere advises the Beast.

Above: In the Beast's lair, Belle discovers an enchanted rose.

Below: The enraged Beast catches Belle and snatches the rose away.

Above: The household objects brace themselves for the attack of
Gaston and the townspeople.

Below: Lumiere rescues the pretty feather duster during the fray.

the tower stairs. He shuffled down the corridor to Belle's door and paused. Now it was *his* turn to gather up courage.

When he opened the door, Belle was on the ground, her head in her hands. She looked up at him with tearful eyes. "I'll never see him again—and you didn't even let me say good-bye!"

The Beast frowned. He hadn't seen this kind of behaviour before. He didn't know people could care so much for one another. "I'll show you to your room," he growled. He walked back into the corridor, snatching up Lumiere in his thick hand.

"My room?" Belle was confused. She thought the Beast wanted to keep her in the tower. She followed him down the stairs and through a long maze of corridors. They both remained silent, until Lumiere could stand it no longer. "*Say* something to her," he whispered to the Beast.

The Beast felt butterflies in his stomach. "I . . . um, hope you'll like it here," he finally said to Belle. Quickly, he looked back at Lumiere for approval.

Lumiere smiled. "Go on," he urged.

"The castle's your home now, so you can go anywhere you like," the Beast said. He thought a moment then added, "Except the West Wing."

"What's in . . . ," Belle began to ask.

Before she could finish, the Beast whirled around angrily. "It's forbidden!"

Lumiere groaned to himself. The Beast wasn't exactly charming Belle.

They walked in silence again until they reached a large guest room. The Beast opened the door, and Belle walked in cautiously.

"If you need anything, my servants will attend to you," the Beast said.

"Invite her to dinner!" Lumiere whispered to him.

"Oh." The Beast nodded, then turned back to Belle. "You'll . . . um, join me for dinner."

But Belle wanted nothing to do with him. Silently, coldly, she pushed the door closed.

But the Beast stopped the door with his hand. There was fury in his eyes, the fury of a person who had never been disobeyed in his life. In a gruff, threatening voice, he said, "That's not a request!"

Belle slammed the door in his face. The Beast snarled and stomped away.

Lumiere sighed with frustration. This love affair was not getting off to a good start.

Back in the village, in a noisy tavern, Gaston was doing what he did best—bragging. He was bragging about his hunting, about his eating, and about his drinking.

He only stopped bragging once, when the tavern door swung open with a loud WHACK!

The tavern fell silent. Everyone watched as a filthy,

wet man stumbled in from the snow. At first no one recognized him.

"Help!" he cried out, his face pale with terror. "He's got her! He's got Belle locked up in his castle!"

Laughter filled the tavern. "It's crazy old Maurice!" one of Gaston's friends yelled.

"Slow down, Maurice," Gaston said. "Who's got Belle locked up?"

"A horrible, monstrous beast!" Maurice replied. "You've got to help me!"

"All right, old man." Gaston said. "We'll help you." With a wink at his friends, he pointed to the door.

Two of the men lifted Maurice by his arms, walked him to the door, and tossed him outside. As they slammed the door behind him, the tavern crowd hooted and cheered.

But Gaston grew serious. He pulled Lefou aside and said, softly, "Crazy as he is, that old man may be of use to us, Lefou. I have just thought of a plan, a plan that will make Belle my bride!"

With a sinister grin, he whispered his plan to Lefou.

Maurice ran frantically through the village streets. "Please help me!" he shouted to everyone he saw. "My daughter has been captured by a beast!"

Everyone ignored him. "Old Maurice has finally

lost his marbles," they all thought as they walked away.

As the snow continued. Maurice sank to his knees in the street. He raised his head upwards and gave one last, desperate cry: "Will no one help me?"

But the only answer was a harsh, whistling wind. Maurice was all alone.

And he knew poor Belle was doomed.

6

$\mathcal{B}$elle threw herself on her bed and sobbed.
The mattress was soft, with a beautiful silk
bed cover that matched the curtains. Everything in
the room was the finest she'd ever seen, from the
carved wooden night table, to the handwoven rug, to
the large wardrobe near the bed.

But to Belle, none of that mattered. The room was a
prison. No matter how beautiful it was, she could
never consider it home. If the Beast was going to keep
her from her father and the things she loved forever,
then she would hate him and his castle forever.

"And I will never have dinner with him!" she
vowed to herself. "Even if he is the only other living
thing in the castle."

A sudden knock on the door interrupted her
thoughts. "Who is it?" she asked.

"Mrs. Potts, dear," a voice said. "I thought you
might like some tea."

So there *were* some other people in the castle, Belle

thought. The voice sounded friendly enough, so she opened the door.

But there was no one there—no person, that is. Just a teapot, who happily walked right in. Behind her skipped a little chipped teacup.

Belle gasped. She backed away, right into the wardrobe.

"Careful!" the wardrobe said.

Belle spun around, and gasped again. The wardrobe had a face, just as the teapot and cup did. They were alive—all of them! "This . . . this is impossible!" Belle said, sitting on the bed.

"I know it is," Wardrobe said, "but here we are!"

The teacup looked up at the teapot and said, "I told you she was pretty, Mama. Didn't I?"

"All right, Chip," Mrs. Potts answered. "Now hold still." Chip stood next to her obediently, and she carefully poured some tea into him.

Smiling with excitement, Chip hopped over to Belle. "Slowly now," Mrs. Potts called out. "Don't spill!"

Belle smiled. Chip was sweet. "Thank you," she said, picking him up and taking a sip.

"That tickles!" said Chip with a giggle.

"You know, my dear," Mrs. Potts said, "changing places with your father was a very brave thing to do."

"We all think so," Wardrobe agreed, sitting next to Belle on the bed.

Belle cast her eyes downwards. "But now I've lost my father, my dreams—everything!"

"It'll turn out all right in the end, you'll see," Mrs. Potts said gently. Then, turning to Chip, she added, "Come now! I almost forgot there's a supper to get on the table!"

As Mrs. Potts and Chip scurried out of the door, Wardrobe pulled a long, silky gown from one of her drawers. "Ah, you'll look ravishing in this at dinner," she said.

"That's very kind of you, but I'm not going to dinner," Belle answered.

"Oh, but you must!" Wardrobe insisted.

Just then, Cogsworth appeared in the bedroom doorway. "Ahem!" he said, clearing his throat. "Dinner is served!"

But Belle was not going to budge from that room, even if every object in the castle came and begged. Her answer was no!

Snow fell outside the dining room windows. The table was set with the finest china. Mrs. Potts had come out of the kitchen to reassure the Beast, and she sat with Lumiere on the mantel over a roaring fire. They watched the Beast pace back and forth.

"What's taking her so long?" the Beast growled.

"Try to be patient, sir," Mrs. Potts said.

"Master," Lumiere added, "have you thought that

perhaps this girl could be the one to break the spell?"

"Of course I have!" the Beast roared. "I'm not a fool! But it's no use. She's so beautiful and I'm . . . well, look at me!"

"You must help her see past all that," Mrs. Potts said.

"I don't know how," the Beast replied sadly. "And the worst thing is that the rose has already started to wilt."

"Well, you can start by making yourself more presentable," Mrs. Potts said. "Straighten up. Try to act like a gentleman."

"Give her a dashing smile," Lumiere suggested.

"But don't let your fangs scare her," Mrs. Potts added.

"Impress her with your delightful wit!" Lumiere said with excitement. "Shower her with compliments."

"But be gentle," Mrs. Potts said, "and sincere."

"And above all," they said together, "you must control your temper!"

KNOCK! KNOCK! KNOCK!

Someone was at the door. "Here she is!" cried Lumiere. The Beast ran a paw through his hair and tried to smile. The door flew open.

But it was only Cogsworth.

"Well, where is she?" the Beast demanded.

"Uh . . who?" Cogsworth said nervously. "Oh, ha

34

ha! The girl, you mean! Well, she's in the process of . . . uh, circumstances being what they are . . ."

The Beast glared at him impatiently. There was no way out for Cogsworth. He had to tell the truth. "She's not coming," he said, his voice a frightened squeak.

"RRRRRRRRAAAGGGGHHHH!" the Beast roared, bolting out of the room. He bounded up the stairs to Belle's room with Lumiere, Cogsworth, and Mrs. Potts running behind.

"You come out or I'll break the door down!" he bellowed, banging at her door.

"I'm not hungry!" Belle shouted from inside.

"Master," Cogsworth said carefully, "please attempt to be a gentleman."

The Beast's nostrils flared with anger, but he knew Cogsworth was right. He took a deep breath. "It would give me great pleasure if you would join me for dinner," he said through gritted teeth.

"No, thank you," Belle's voice shot back.

That was all the Beast could take. "Fine!" he yelled. "Then go ahead and starve!" He whirled around to face Cogsworth and Lumiere. "If she won't eat with me, then she won't eat at all!" he roared.

As he stormed away, Mrs. Potts remarked, "Oh, dear. That didn't go very well, did it?"

Cogsworth threw up his hands and sighed. "We might as well go downstairs and start cleaning up.

35

Lumiere, stand guard here and inform me if there's the slightest change."

"My eyes will never leave the door," Lumiere replied.

The Beast didn't stop until he'd reached his lair in the West Wing. He threw his door open and clomped into the room, muttering to himself, "I ask nicely but she refuses! What does she want me to do, beg?"

He grabbed the magic mirror off his dressing table, the mirror that allowed him to see anywhere he desired. "Show me the girl!" he demanded.

Slowly a vision of Belle's room appeared. Belle was sitting on her bed, arms crossed in anger. Wardrobe walked over to her and said, "The master's really not all that bad once you get to know him. Why don't you give him a chance?"

"He's ruined my life!" Belle replied. "I don't want to have anything to do with him!"

The Beast didn't want to hear any more. As he put the mirror down, his eyes filled with sadness. "She'll never see me as anything but a monster," he said to himself. "It's hopeless."

Before his last word was finished, another petal fell from the rose. The Beast shuddered as it fluttered to the tabletop.

7

*L*ater that night, Belle sneaked out of her room. There was no one standing guard but she could hear giggles down the hall. Glancing to her left, she saw Lumiere flirting with a pretty feather duster.

She tiptoed down the hall. She was starving. She hadn't wanted to eat dinner with the Beast, but that didn't mean she wanted to starve!

She walked quietly down the stairs. It wasn't hard finding the kitchen. Down a long hallway she could hear the clanking of pots and pans behind a door.

Slowly she pushed the door open. For a moment, everyone in the kitchen froze. Cogsworth was there, along with Mrs. Potts, and a very angry-looking stove.

Cogsworth was the first to speak. "Splendid to see you, mademoiselle," he said, with a deep bow. "I am Cogsworth, head of the household.

Imediately, Lumiere ran in, out of breath and

looking guilty. Cogsworth gave him a sharp glare and said, "And that is Lumiere."

Lumiere reached for Belle's hand and tried to kiss it, but Cogsworth slapped him away. "If there's anything we can do to make your stay more comfortable . . ." Cogsworth said in an unconvincing tone.

"I *am* a little hungry," Belle replied.

Mrs. Potts's eyes lit up. "Are you?" she said. Turning to the others, she called out, "Hear that? Stoke the fire! Take out the silverware! Wake the china!"

"No!" Cogsworth shouted. "Remember what the master said. If she doesn't eat with him, she doesn't eat at all!"

But no one listened to Cogsworth. Instead, all the objects flew into action. The stove began cooking on all burners. Platters full of good food leapt into the oven.

Smiling, Lumiere gracefully escorted Belle into the dining room. "Mademoiselle, it is with deep pride and great pleasure that we welcome you," he said grandly. "And now we invite you to relax and pull up a chair as the dining room proudly presents—your dinner!"

He acted like the master of ceremonies at a show, and that's exactly what Belle saw: a show. She watched in wonder as the plates, platters, and silverware all danced and sang on the table. Then a chair slid underneath Belle, and pushed her towards the table. The first course was served.

The kitchen door swung open time and time again. Each time, Belle's mouth watered. And each time, a platter of food came out, more delicious than the last.

The name of each dish was announced in song and dance. There were hot hors d'oeuvres, beef ragout, cheese soufflé, and a dessert of pie and flaming pudding. It was a lot of food, but Belle managed to clean every plate. She'd never had a dinner so delicious, nor seen a show so unusual!

When it was all over, she burst into applause. Even Cogsworth got into the spirit of things, and danced his heart out. He and Lumiere and the rest of the objects all bowed deeply to her, grinning with pleasure.

"Bravo!" Belle exclaimed. "That was wonderful! I've never been in an enchanted castle before. I'd like to look around now, if that's all right."

Cogsworth snapped out of his good mood. "Wait a second! I'm not sure that's a good idea. The master . . ."

"Perhaps you'd like to take me," Belle said to Cogsworth. "I'm sure *you* know everything there is to know about the castle."

"Well, actually," Cogsworth said, his chest puffing with pride, "I do!"

Strutting proudly, he led her on a tour of the castle.

He talked and talked, explaining every single detail in every single room. Lumiere followed behind, but he quickly became bored. He looked around, humming and singing to himself.

As they neared the West Wing, Cogsworth and Lumiere realized something terrible. Belle had disappeared.

"Mademoiselle?" Cogsworth called out.

Out of the corner of his eye, he spotted Belle moving up a dark set of stairs.

Instantly, Cogsworth and Lumiere raced ahead of Belle and blocked the way.

"What's up there?" Belle asked.

"Nothing!" Cogsworth replied. "Absolutely nothing of interest in the West Wing. Dusty, dull, and very boring."

"Ah, so this is the West Wing," Belle said, remembering the Beast's warning. "I wonder what he's hiding up there?"

She started to take a step up, but Cogsworth didn't budge. "Perhaps mademoiselle would like to see something else," he said desperately. "We have tapestries, gardens, a library . . ."

"You have a library?" Belle asked.

"Oh, yes, indeed!" Cogsworth said. "With more books than you'll ever be able to read in a lifetime!"

He and Lumiere led her back downstairs. She followed, as Cogsworth went on and on, "We have books on every subject, by every author who ever set pen to paper . . ."

The truth was that Belle did want to see the library, but her curiosity about the West Wing was getting the better of her. She lagged further and further behind her two hosts, then stopped.

They were so involved in describing the library that they didn't notice. Belle spun around and ran back to the West Wing stairs.

She raced up the stairs, taking them two at a time. But when she got to the top, she stopped. Before her, a long, gloomy corridor stretched into darkness. Its walls were lined with mirrors, each one broken. Slowly she walked past them into the deep shadows.

At the end of the corridor was an enormous wooden door. Above it, two hideous carved faces sneered at her. They seemed to be saying, "Stay away! Stay away!"

Belle took a deep breath. She pushed the door, and it creaked open.

Belle's eyes widened. A gasp caught in her throat. The room was like nothing she'd ever seen before. Every corner, every surface was covered with filth. Vines grew into the room from an open window and twisted around broken furniture, cracked mirrors, and ripped paintings. Cupboard doors hung crookedly from torn hinges, and bed coverings lay in a dirty pile against one wall. In a corner was a stack of bones that looked as though they had been chewed on.

Belle's stomach began to churn. As she walked into the room, she shivered. "Is this where he lives?" she thought.

A painting on the wall caught her attention. It was a portrait of a young boy. Belle thought there was something familiar about his eyes, but she couldn't be sure. The painting had five deep slashes across it, as if the Beast had ripped it with his claws.

But then Belle noticed the rose. Although it was drooping and most of its petals had fallen off, it seemed to shimmer. She went closer, reaching out her hand towards it. The petals were so delicate, so beautiful.

Belle was so enchanted by the rose, she didn't notice the hulking shadow of the Beast in the open window.

8

*AA*ARGGGGHHH!" the Beast roared as he leapt in front of Belle.

Belle screamed and backed away. Her trembling fingers never touched the rose.

The Beast stomped toward her, smashing everything in his way. "I warned you never to come here!" he shouted, hurling a heavy chair as if it were made of paper. "Do you realize what you could have done?"

"I didn't mean any harm," Belle pleaded.

The Beast answered by throwing a table against a wall. "Get out!" he bellowed. "Get out!"

Belle wasted no time. She got out, all right—out of the castle. Promise or no promise, she was *not* going to stay there!

Philippe was waiting outside, exactly where she'd left him. She hopped on and shouted, "Take me home!"

Philippe's hooves thundered against the frozen earth. In seconds they were out of the castle grounds

43

and into the woods. Belle felt a rush of happiness.

But as soon as they plunged into the woods, that feeling ended. The forest was every bit as dark and thick as she remembered it. Philippe had to slow to a walk, dodging branches that hung down like long claws. In the mist, he couldn't see more than a few feet in front of them.

But there was no mistaking the eyes.

The yellow, fierce eyes of the wolf pack.

With angry growls, the wolves attacked Philippe's heels. Philippe whinnied and reared onto his hind legs.

With a crash, Belle tumbled onto the forest floor. One wolf spotted her. Then another.

The wolves lunged at her. She scrambled away, grabbing a thick branch. Her heart raced with fear as she swung the branch at them.

They danced around the branch, stalking closer. Belle tried to back away, but as she did, she tripped on a tangled root. A jolt of pain shot through her ankle, and Belle fell to the ground.

The wolves pounced. Belle felt their claws on her neck. There was nothing she could do now but scream.

9

Then, suddenly, someone pulled the wolves off Belle.

She could still hear them snarling behind her, only now they were attacking her rescuer! She was startled when she saw who it was.

It was the Beast!

She pulled herself to her feet and ran to Philippe's side. Together they watched helplessly as the Beast fought the furious animals. The wolves slashed him with their teeth and claws, and the Beast howled in pain.

But he was more than a match for them. One by one, he grabbed each wolf and hurled it away. The clever ones slunk away when they realized it was a losing battle.

Soon the Beast stood alone. His face was twisted in agony. He tried to walk towards Belle, but after a few steps, he fell to the ground with a groan.

Belle looked to her left. The road to escape was

narrow, but she and Philippe were free to take it. They were free to gallop back to her house, free to leave the Beast and his horrible world behind.

The Beast moaned. He glanced up at Belle with a look of shock and pain.

And Belle realized at that moment that she couldn't leave. Not while the Beast lay wounded in the snow.

"Help me take him back, Philippe," she said softly.

She led her faithful horse to the Beast and helped him to his feet. Together they trudged back to the castle. The Beast limped along, leaning against Philippe.

In the castle's grand hall, Belle nursed the Beast's wounds. He squirmed in pain. "If you hadn't run away, this wouldn't have happened!" he said angrily.

"If you hadn't frightened me, I wouldn't have run away!" Belle replied, cleaning one of his cuts with a wet cloth.

"Well, you shouldn't have been in the West Wing!" the Beast snapped.

"And you should learn to control your temper!" Belle said. They glared at each other for a long moment. Then their eyes dropped. Belle pulled her scarf off and began wrapping it around one of the wounds. "Now hold still. This may hurt a little."

The Beast gritted his teeth and didn't move. Finally, Belle said what she'd been meaning to say since they were in the woods. "By the way, thank you for saving my life."

"You're welcome," the Beast said with a smile.

Pain or no pain, he suddenly felt very good inside.

At that same moment, Gaston and Lefou were walking towards Belle's cottage with a strange man dressed entirely in black. His name was Monsieur D'Arque, and he was tall and skinny with a sharp nose and small eyes. He was the head of an insane asylum called Maison des Loons, and was part of Gaston's evil plan.

For a bag of gold, he had agreed to throw Maurice into his asylum—unless Belle would agree to marry Gaston.

What they didn't know was that Maurice had left the cottage to find Belle. At that moment he was entering the woods on foot.

When Gaston found that the cottage was empty, he turned to his partners and said, "They have to come back sometime, and when they do, we'll be ready for them. Lefou, stay here and keep watch."

Lefou waited by the stairway. Gaston and Monsieur d'Argue walked slowly back towards the village to find out where Maurice and Belle were. "*No one* will stop me from having Belle this time!" proclaimed Gaston angrily.

Snow had fallen during the night, covering the tangled vines and the broken statues. The blanket of white made the castle grounds almost cheerful.

Since the evening of the wolf attack, the Beast was a lot more cheerful, too. And it was all because of Belle. Her recent kindness and attention had brought out the best in him.

From his bedroom window, he watched Belle walk Philippe, and he thought to himself, "I want to do something for her."

He decided to give her a special gift, and with the help of Cogsworth and Lumiere, he thought of a good one. But it would take a lot of planning—and a lot of cleaning.

After hours of preparation, the gift was ready. The Beast led Belle down a hallway and stopped in front of a set of double doors. "I want to show you something," he said, "but first you have to close your eyes. It's a surprise."

Belle did as she was told. The Beast opened the door, then took her hand. He led her inside a dark room with a high ceiling. "Can I open my eyes now?" she said.

"Not yet," he said. Letting go of her hand, he went to a window and pulled back a curtain. Sunlight poured into the room.

"Now," the Beast said.

Belle opened her eyes, and they sparkled with

delight. It was a beautiful library, stacked with shelves and shelves of books. At one end, there was a roaring fire with a stuffed leather armchair in front of it.

"I can't believe it!" Belle said in awe. "I've never seen so many books in my life!"

The Beast smiled. "You like it? It's yours," he said.

"Oh, thank you so much!" Belle exclaimed.

Hiding around a corner, Cogsworth and Lumiere smiled at each other. Maybe the spell could be broken after all.

Over the next few days, things began to change between Belle and the Beast. They were becoming friends! Belle learned a lot about the Beast, too. He didn't know how to eat with a knife and fork, so she taught him. He didn't know how to read, so she read to him. She taught him how to feed birds and how to play in the snow.

"She doesn't shudder when she touches my paw any more," noticed the Beast.

"There's something about him I didn't see before" thought Belle. "I thought he was ugly and cruel, but now he seems sweet and gentle."

The Beast was actually learning how to have fun for the first time in his life. He was discovering feelings inside himself, tender feelings he didn't know he could have. Feelings for Belle.

It wasn't long before the Beast realized something shocking: He was in love with Belle, and he knew he had to do something about it.

He had to tell her.

But how? Not just any old way. He had to create a magical moment, sweep her off her feet. He would invite Belle for a night of dancing in the ballroom!

He was delighted when she agreed. On the night of the dance, the Beast did some things he had never done before. He bathed himself, dressed up, and even combed his mane.

As he walked to the ballroom stairs to wait for Belle, the Beast looked completely different. His mane shone in the light; his outfit was elegant. Lumiere provided romantic candlelight, and Mrs. Potts sang a love song.

When Belle appeared at the top of the ballroom stairs in a shimmering gold gown, the Beast felt himself freeze. He was stunned by her beauty, and he was also very nervous.

He walked up the stairs, took her hand, and with a gallant smile, he escorted her down. Then he whirled her into dance position. He lifted his huge, hairy foot and took the first step—and practically mashed her toes.

The Beast was horrified. He'd gone to all this trouble to create a perfect evening, but it wasn't going to work. He was so clumsy!

Belle didn't even frown. She gave him a warm smile and did what she had been doing for the last few days—she taught him.

The Beast slowly picked up the steps, and before long they were sweeping gracefully across the dance floor.

Soon, laughing and out of breath, they decided to go out on to the balcony. As the Beast opened the glass door, cool air rushed in. The night was still and the ground glimmered with snow in the moonlight. Above, thousands of stars winked at them.

As she looked up, Belle sighed and smiled.

And the Beast knew that this was the moment of truth. "Uh, Belle," he said softly. "Are you . . . happy here with me?"

Belle thought a moment. She had to admit that she was happier than she had expected to be. "Yes," she answered.

But the Beast could sense sadness in her eyes. "What is it?" he asked.

Belle looked at the Beast. She was close to tears. "If only I could see my father again. Just for a moment," she said. "I miss him so much."

The Beast returned her gaze for a long time. He had the power to let her see her father. And he realized now that he would do anything for her. "There is a way," he said.

Without another word, he led her into the West

Wing and up to his room. There, he took the magic mirror from his table and handed it to her. "The mirror will show you anything," he said. "Anything you wish to see."

Belle held it up. "I'd like to see my father, please," she whispered.

The mirror began to glow. An image appeared, dark and blurry. As it became clearer, Belle could see trees and bushes. It was the forest, and there was something moving through it. Something slow and hunched, like a wounded animal.

When the being looked up to the sky, Belle recognized her father. "Belle," he called out, his voice cracked and hoarse. Maurice fell to his knees, shaking and coughing.

"Papa!" Belle screamed. She turned to the Beast with panic in her eyes. "He's sick! He may be dying! And he's all alone!"

The Beast swallowed hard. As he looked at Belle's tear-streaked face and saw the pain that was ripping her apart, his heart skipped a beat. He could feel her pain as if it were his own. "Her father needs her now, but so do I," thought the Beast.

He glanced towards his table and saw two shriveled petals clinging to the dying rose. Soon they would fall off. If he let Belle go now, he would never know if she loved him and the spell would never be broken. He would remain a hideous beast forever.

But as he turned and looked into Belle's eyes again, he knew there was only one thing to do.

"You must go to him," he said, slowly speaking the words he knew would seal his doom forever.

Belle stared at him in disbelief. "You mean, I'm free?"

The Beast tried hard to keep his voice steady, without emotion. "I release you. You're no longer my prisoner."

Belle gripped his hand joyfully. "Oh, thank you!" She began to run out the door, but turned back when she realized she was still holding the mirror.

The Beast shook his head. "Take it with you," he said, "so you'll always have a way to look back . . . and remember me."

Belle clutched the mirror to her chest. "Thank you for understanding how much he needs me," she said.

"I need you just as much!" was what the Beast wanted to say. The words welled up inside his heart and went racing right up to his mouth.

But he never said them. Instead, he just nodded.

Belle touched his hand briefly and ran out, her gown flowing behind her.

The Beast stood on his balcony. He watched Belle emerge from the castle's front door, mount Philippe and gallop away, the moonlight glinting in her silken hair.

When they were gone, the Beast did something he hadn't done since he was a boy.

He threw back his head and howled, with a pain that cut to the bottom of his heart.

10

" Thank goodness he's still alive!" was all Belle could think when she found her father in the snow. He was soaked, he had a fever, and he didn't recognize her. But he was alive.

She managed to get him onto Philippe, and together they galloped at top speed through the snow-covered forest. All the way home, Maurice kept repeating things. "It should have been me!" he muttered, and "I'm not a thief!" and "Run, Belle! Run!"

When they got to their cottage, Belle instantly put Maurice to bed and he fell into a long, deep sleep. For hours, she mopped his brow and held his hand. Belle worried that he would never recover, never recognize her again.

Finally he awoke with a moan. "It should have been me . . . me!" His eyes flickered. He gave Belle a blank stare. Then, slowly, he smiled. "Belle?"

Belle was filled with relief. He knew who she was! "It's all right, Papa," she said. "I'm home."

Joyous tears filled Maurice's eyes. He sat up and threw his arms around his daughter. They hugged and laughed and cried. "I missed you so much!" Belle said.

"But how did you escape the Beast?" Maurice asked.

"He let me go," Belle said softly.

Maurice was shocked. "That horrible beast?"

"He's different now, Papa," Belle said with a sigh. "He's changed somehow."

Just then Belle noticed a small movement out of the corner of her eye. There was something moving in her saddlebag. She flipped open a flap, and there was Chip, Mrs. Pott's teacup son! He gave her a guilty smile.

Belle smiled back. "Oh . . . a stowaway."

RAP! RAP! RAP! RAP!

Belle and Maurice were both startled by the loud knocking on the door. With a shrug, Belle covered Chip again, went to the door, and opened it.

There stood a tall, skinny man dressed in black. Behind him was a wooden wagon with the words Maison Des Loons on the side. A crowd, led by Lefou, was gathering next to the wagon.

"May I . . . help you?" Belle asked.

"I am Monsieur d'Arque," the man said. "I've come to collect your father."

"He was raving like a lunatic outside the tavern!"

56

Lefou added. "We all heard him, didn't we?"

Most of the crowd mumbled in agreement. A few men, dressed in the white uniforms of the Maison des Loons, stepped towards the house.

"My father's not mad!" Belle said, standing firmly in the doorway. "I won't let you take him!"

Maurice walked up behind Belle to see what was going on. As soon as Lefou saw him he shouted, "Maurice, tell us again. How big *was* that beast?"

"Well, I'd say eight—no, more like ten feet tall!" Maurice answered seriously.

The crowd hooted with laughter. "You don't get much madder than that!" Lefou shouted.

Forcing their way past Belle, Monsieur d'Arque's men grabbed Maurice and pulled him outside.

"No!" Belle screamed, running after them. "You can't do this!"

Suddenly Gaston stepped out of the shadows and right into Belle's path. With a calm smile, he said, "Poor Belle. It's a shame about your father."

"You know he's not mad!" Belle snapped, eyeing Gaston with suspicion.

"Hmmm . . ." Gaston pretended to think hard. "I might be able to clear up this little misunderstanding, *if* . . ." His voice trailed off.

"If what?" Belle asked.

"If you marry me," Gaston answered.

Belle stepped back in shock. He was grinning at

57

her, certain that his plan had worked.

"Never!" she said.

Gaston shrugged. "Have it your way." He waved at Monsieur D'Arque's men. "Take him away."

Belle raced back into the house and brought out the enchanted mirror. Standing on the front steps, she shouted, "My father's not mad and I can prove it!"

The crowd stared at her. Monsieur d'Argue's men stopped. Gaston looked up, worried.

"Show me the Beast!" Belle said to the mirror.

The mirror glowed. The crowd gasped. Slowly the Beast's image appeared. He paced the balcony in torment. Then, raising his head, he let out a blood-curdling howl.

People in the crowd screamed and ran away. Monsieur d'Arque's men dropped Maurice and quickly rode off in their wagon. "Is he dangerous?" someone yelled out.

Belle looked tenderly at the Beast's image. She knew he was howling from a broken heart. "Oh, no. I know he looks vicious, but he's really kind and gentle. He's . . . my friend."

Gaston was furious that his plan had failed. He was also very jealous. "If I didn't know better," he said to Belle, "I'd think you had feelings for that monster."

"He's no monster, Gaston!" Belle snapped. "*You* are!"

Gaston grabbed the mirror. He whirled around to

58

the crowd, red with fury. "She's as mad as the old man!" he announced. "The Beast will come after your children in the night! He'll wreck our village!"

The crowd began to panic, shouting angrily.

"No!" Belle protested.

But Gaston kept on. "We're not safe until his head is mounted on my wall! I say we kill the Beast!"

Bell tried to stop Gaston, but he signalled to his friends. "Lock them in the cellar!" he ordered.

"Get your hands off me!" Belle screamed.

"We can't have them running off to warn the creature!" Gaston yelled to the frightend crowd. So Gaston's men forced Belle and Maurice down the cellar steps.

The door slammed shut over their heads. The last thing Belle saw was Gaston leading the crowd towards the forest. They were yelling over and over, "Kill the Beast! Kill the Beast!"

11

$\mathcal{L}$umiere, Cogsworth, and Mrs. Potts were moping in the castle foyer when they heard voices outside.

"Is it she?" Mrs. Potts asked excitedly.

They all ran to the window, hoping to see Belle. But their happy expressions turned to shock. It wasn't Belle at all. It was Gaston and his angry mob!

"Invaders!" Lumiere cried out.

The castle objects began running into the room from all directions. "Barricade the door!" Cogsworth ordered. "Mrs. Potts, warn the master!"

BOOOOOOOM! The castle shook as the mob attacked the door with a battering ram. Cogsworth and the other objects piled themselves against the door.

Mrs. Potts sprinted to the Beast's lair, where he was sitting silently. His head was bowed, his body slumped.

"Master, the castle is under attack," Mrs. Potts said.

The Beast looked up. His eyes were lined with red, as if he'd been crying. "It doesn't matter now," he said. "Just let them come."

"But Master . . .", Mrs. Potts began.

BOOOOOOOM! The sound of another battering ram attack cut her off. "Kill the Beast!" came the chant from the crowd. "Kill the Beast!"

With a deafening crash, the door fell in and the objects scattered.

But when Gaston's mob barged in, they stopped short. They knew someone had to have been holding back the door, but now the room was empty. All they could see was a candelabra, a mantel clock, and a few other objects.

"Something fishy's going on around here," Lefou said. He cautiously crept closer and closer to Lumiere.

With a sudden jab, Lumiere poked him in the eyes.

'YEOUCHHH!" Lefou screamed.

'CHAAAAARGE!" Lumiere bellowed.

The battle was on! Gaston's men couldn't believe what they were seeing. Candelabras, clocks, dishes, fireplace tongs, footstools, and brushes—all fighting!

As his men fought, Gaston slipped further into the castle. He would find the Beast himself.

Meanwhile, outside the cottage, Maurice's invention stood on top of a gentle hill. It was a large contraption, a maze of ropes, levers, pulleys, wheels, bells, and whistles. Only Maurice knew what it was supposed to do. Only Maurice knew how to work it.

But there was someone else walking around it at that moment. Someone very small, and very smart. Someone who could sneak out of the house unnoticed.

It was Chip!

He looked the contraption over once, twice. He turned a few knobs, pulled a few levers, gave it a little nudge . . .

WHIIIRRRR . . . BONK . . . BLEEP . . .

The invention coughed to life! It began to roll forwards. Chip jumped up and down with glee. It rolled to the left, then to the right, then directly towards the cellar door.

Maurice and Belle both heard a loud rumble. Maurice peeked through the window in the cellar door and saw the contraption barreling towards them. "Belle, look out!" he shouted.

They both ducked away just as the contraption came bursting through the cellar door. On it, hanging from a small lever, was Chip.

"You did it, little teacup!" Belle shouted happily.

"Let's go!" Maurice said.

They ran outside. Philippe saw them and whinnied joyfully.

"Philippe, my old friend," Maurice called out. "Take us to the castle!"

In the castle, the battle raged on. Gaston's men stormed the kitchen and the dining room. Everywhere the objects rose up to defend their home.

But Gaston was in a quieter place, upstairs, just outside the Beast's lair. He inched closer to the closed door and pulled an arrow out of his quiver. Lashing out with his foot, he kicked the door down.

The Beast slowly turned from his place at the window. When he saw Gaston, he didn't react at all. Nothing mattered to him now.

Gaston fired an arrow. It sliced through the air and landed firmly in the Beast's shoulder.

"RRRAAAAAHHHHHRRRRGGGHHH!" The Beast shrieked in agony and fell to the floor.

He crawled slowly across the floor and out onto the balcony. Gaston ran to him and gave him a sharp kick. With another howl of pain, the Beast tumbled over the balcony railing. He landed on the smooth, sloping slates of the castle roof.

"Get up!" Gaston shouted, as he grabbed a club that hung on the wall.

The Beast tried, but only got as far as his knees. Rain had begun to fall, making the roof wet and slippery.

Gaston climbed out on to the roof and held the club

high. With a mighty blow, he brought it down on the Beast's back.

The Beast howled again and collapsed. As he slid down the side of the roof, Gaston repeated, "Get up!"

He hit the Beast again and again. The Beast tried to rise, but he was too weak. He was now dangerously close to the edge of the roof. A few more inches and he would fall off. A few more inches and it would be all over. He would never again have to think of Belle, his lost love.

As Gaston raised his club for the final blow, the Beast caught one last glimpse through his window. He saw the rose, with one petal left.

"NOOOOOOO!" a scream rang out from below.

With his last ounce of strength, the Beast turned his head. The voice was familiar. It made his heart pump wildly. It made his every sense quicken. Could it be?

Yes. It was Belle. She was racing towards the castle on her horse, along with her father. The Beast felt himself come alive again, as if waking from a nightmare.

Gaston glared at the back of the Beast's head. "YEEEAAAHH!" he shrieked at the top of his lungs, and brought the club down as hard as he could.

12

The Beast spun around. Gaston's club was coming towards him at lightning speed. There was no time to think. The Beast's hand darted out. His palm smacked into the side of the club, and stopped it in mid-air.

Gaston was stunned. He backed away as the Beast slowly rose to his feet. The Beast's shadow seemed to swallow Gaston. He flailed wildly with his club again and again, but the Beast blocked it each time.

Roaring with fury, the Beast stalked after him. With a swipe of his long arm, he whacked the club out of Gaston's hand.

Below them, there was a clatter of hooves on the castle stairs. Philippe had galloped right into the castle!

But the Beast hardly heard it. He was burning with outrage. He wanted revenge!

The Beast lunged forward and grabbed Gaston by

the neck. With a fruious roar, he hoisted Gaston into the air.

"Let me go!" Gaston pleaded. "Please . . . I'll do anything!"

"Kill him!" The words raced through the Beast's mind. He grabbed Gaston with his other arm, twisted Gaston's body, and prepared to break his neck.

Then he stopped.

Maybe it was the terror in Gaston's eyes. Maybe it was Gaston's helplessness. Maybe the time spent with Belle had made the Beast softhearted.

But whatever the reason, he let Gaston down and said simply, "Get out."

Then he saw Belle. She stood in his room, looking out the window. Her face was pale, her hair wet and messy from her wild ride. She was out of breath and looked exhausted.

But she was the most beautiful sight the Beast could ever imagine.

He began to limp towards her. She smiled warmly and held out her arms. But suddenly her body went tense. A look of panic shot through her face. "Beast!" she screamed, as she pointed over his shoulder.

It was too late. Gaston was in mid-air, lunging towards him with a knife. By the time the Beast could react, the knife was squarely between his shoulders.

His agonized roar echoed into the night. He

staggered around and faced Gaston with a look of horror and anger.

Gaston went white with fear. He took a step back without looking and his foot landed in a gutter. He tried to pull it out, but he couldn't take his eyes off the Beast.

The Beast stumbled forward. Gaston yanked his foot out and lost his balance. Whirling his arms like a windmill, he fell and slid to the edge of the roof.

And then, in a flash, he was gone. Only his scream remained as he plunged over the side.

The Beast turned back to face Belle. He climbed slowly onto the balcony, tried to plant his feet, and fell.

Belle ran to him and cradled him in her arms.

In spite of the pain, he managed a weak smile. "You . . . came back," he said, gasping with pain. "At least . . . I got to see you one last time . . ."

Belle fought back tears. "Don't talk like that," she said. "You'll be all right."

Suddenly there was a sound of clattering footsteps in the Beast's room. Cogsworth, Lumiere, and Mrs Potts ran to the balcony window. They stopped, frozen with shock at the sight of their fallen master.

Behind them, the rose's last petal wavered in the breeze.

"Maybe it's better this way," the Beast said. He was struggling to keep his eyes open.

"No! Please . . . please!" Belle cried out in anguish. Tears flowed down her cheeks and spilled onto the Beast's face. She leaned closer to his limp, wounded body. She planted a tender kiss on his cheek. "I love you!" she cried.

As she spoke, the rose's last petal fell to the table.

13

$\mathcal{F}$or a moment, all was quiet, except for the muffled sounds of Belle's weeping.

Then something remarkable happened. Suddenly the rain began to sparkle and shimmer with light. Then the air began to glow.

The Beast opened his eyes. He felt a healing warmth throughout his body. He looked at his hands. The hair was disappearing! Long, strong fingers remained where a mangled paw had just been. He gasped, then reached up to touch his face.

It was smooth! And his wounds were gone. He felt as healthy and strong as . . . as . . . He could barely bring himself to think the words: "As healthy and strong as a young prince."

Could it be, or was this some sort of dream?

One look at Belle's face was enough to give him an answer. She was staring at him as if she'd never seen him before.

And behind her, glowing magically, the rose was in full bloom!

The Prince rose to his feet. It all came back to him—how it felt to stand perfectly straight, how it felt to be *human*. He hadn't forgotten.

But he was different now. He was taller, older, stronger. And most important, he was looking at the whole world differently. Not with greed and anger and spite, but with kindness, understanding, strength—and love.

"Belle," he said gently. "It's me."

She looked at him, startled for a moment, not knowing what to believe. But there was something about his smile, about the look in his eyes. It *was* the same being with whom she had fallen in love.

With a radiant smile, Belle ran into his arms. And there on the balcony, as the sun peeked over the horizon, they shared a long kiss.

The kiss seemed to bring new magic to the castle. In a swirl of light and colour, Cogsworth turned into a robust man with a mustache. Lumiere became a tall, dashing butler. Mrs. Potts turned into a plump sweet-faced woman.

"The spell is broken!" Cogsworth said, his voice choked with emotion.

The Prince grinned at his faithful servants. He turned briefly from Belle and embraced them. All over the castle, he could hear screams of joy. The

70

objects, from the East Wing to the West Wing, were all becoming the people they once were.

Memories flooded back to the Prince. Memories of a beautiful, shining castle with flags flying and people running about, working, laughing, singing. A lush green meadow. A moat of deep blue water.

The night was lifting—and so were the years of gloom. As the sun rose, the countryside burst into bloom.

But none of it was as lovely as the vision the Prince held in his eyes right then—Belle's smile.

It was a smile that the Prince hoped to be looking at for the rest of his life.

In one last burst of magic, everyone in the castle was whisked into the ballroom. Musicians played, lights twinkled, and the floor shone like a mirror.

The Prince held out his hand, and Belle joined him for a dance. As they swirled around the room, Belle saw happiness in every corner. Mrs. Potts was hugging her little teacups, who were all real, live children, including one with a chipped tooth.

"Chip!" Belle called out, waving to him.

She swirled around again and saw her father, Maurice, looking at everything in awe. He glanced beside him. Wardrobe was now a lovely lady-in-waiting. She winked at him and he blushed.

The footstool, now a happy dog, raced between people's legs as they got up to dance.

Belle laughed. For years, she had thought fairy tales could only be read in books. But as she looked into the adoring eyes of her Prince, she knew that what was happening to her was real. And she knew exactly what the ending to her real-life fairy tale would be.

She and her Prince would live happily ever after.